D0718169

COCK CROW

Poems about life
in the countryside
chosen by

Michael Morpurgo
& Jane Feaver

Illustrated by

Quentin Blake

EGMONT

Farms for City Children aims to enrich the lives and develop the potential of children from an urban area by giving them the opportunity to become farmers for a week on a working farm in the heart of the countryside. The Charity was founded by Clare and Michael Morpurgo almost thirty years ago and now, on three different farms, provides this experience for over 3,000 children a year.

10% of the publisher's proceeds from the sale of each copy of this book shall be donated to Farms for City Children.

First published in Great Britain 2005 by Egmont Books Limited
239 Kensington High Street, London W8 6SA

Selection © 2005 Michael Morpurgo and Jane Feaver
Introduction © 2005 Michael Morpurgo
Illustrations © 2005 Quentin Blake

The editors and illustrator have asserted their moral rights.

ISBN 1 4052 1288 8

1 3 5 7 9 10 8 6 4 2

A CIP catalogue record for this title is available from the British Library

Printed and bound in Singapore

Contents

Introduction

Several hundred years ago in one of the earliest poems in English, an unknown poet wrote the tale of Sir Gawain and the Green Knight. Like me, this writer trod the fields, felt the hot sun and hard rain on his face, watched the seasons come and go. Between us – him then, me now – we wrote this:

'But a whole year does not pass in the twinkle of an eye, not for you, not for me, not for Gawain. Every season must take its time. After all the fun and feasting and frolicking of the New Year is done, then comes unwelcome fish-eating Lent, but even by now the first snowdrops have shown their pretty heads and the cold of winter begun to lose its icy grip. A pale new sun drives away the last of winter's clouds. Primrose and daffodil bring promise of longer days, and grass and leaves grow green again. Blackbirds cackle in budding gardens and woodpeckers knock in hollow trees. The first cuckoo and the first lark tell us for sure it is spring again, and swallows and swifts bring us the hope of summer, skimming low over the hayfields, screeching round our chimney tops. Now we have mornings

of soft valley mists and garden dews. Salmon rise in the rivers, and the gentle breeze of summer touches our cheeks. The earth itself warms with life, feeding the seeds that will soon grow and be feeding us. And all about us we hear now the humming of bees, the crying of lambs, the mewing of soaring buzzards. Soon enough though the harvest calls us to the fields and we must hurry, for we know from the chill in the evenings that autumn is almost upon us. The trees dressed so brightly, so gloriously, in brown and red and gold stand and wait in dread for the rough winds of winter that will soon make stark skeletons of them again. Now we huddle inside once more before our fires and through rattling windows watch the leaves fly and the green of the grass turn grey before our eyes.'

Michael Morpurgo

'And this our life'

And this our life, exempt from public haunt,
Finds tongues in trees, books in the running brooks,
Sermons in stones, and good in everything.

William Shakespeare, from *As You Like It*

The Farmer's Boy

The sun had set behind yon hill,
   Across the dreary moor,
When weary and lame, a boy there came,
   Up to a farmer's door;
'Can you tell me where ever I be,
   One that will me employ.
To plough and sow, to reap and mow
And be a farmer's boy,
And be a farmer's boy?'

The farmer's wife cried, 'Try the lad,
   Let him no longer seek'

'Yes Father, do,' the daughter cried,
    While the tears roll'd down her cheek:
'For those who would work, 'tis hard to want,
    And wander for employ.
Don't let him go, but let him stay,
And be a farmer's boy,
And be a farmer's boy.'

The farmer's boy grew up a man,
    And the good old couple died;
They left the lad the farm they had,
    And the daughter for his bride;
Now the lad which was, and the farm now has,
    Often thinks and smiles with joy.
And will bless the day he came that way
To be a farmer's boy,
To be a farmer's boy.'

Anon

A Lamb in the Storm

But the world is brave.
Eyes squeezed tight shut, she plunges.
Surf goes over the house, dust-bin lids fly.

Ears of owls, hairfine electronics
Are jammed with the sky-disaster.
They anchor their cork-weights, clamped hungry
To trees that struggle to save themselves.

The world's brow
Plunges into blindness and deafness –
Farms and villages cling.

Chunks of the wreck reel past.

But the world
Just about finished,
Stripped and stunned, keeps her battered direction –

She knows who it is, still alive out there,
The castaway voice
Where heaven breaks up in the darkness.

Ted Hughes

Snaw

The Men o the East
Are pykin their geese,
An sen'in their feathers here awa, there awa.

Anon (Scottish)

Bye, Baby Bunting

Bye, baby bunting,
Daddy's gone a-hunting,
Gone to get a rabbit skin
To wrap the baby bunting in.

Anon

Riley

Down in the water-meadows Riley
Spread his wash on the bramble-thorn,
Sat, one foot in the moving water,
Bare as the day that he was born.

Candid was his curling whisker,
Brown his body as an old tree-limb,
Blue his eye as the jay above him
Watching him watch the minjies swim.

Four stout sticks for walls had Riley,
His roof was a rusty piece of tin,
As snug in the lew of a Cornish hedgerow
He watched the seasons out and in.

He paid no rates, he paid no taxes,
His lamp was the moon hung in the tree.
Though many an ache and pain had Riley
He envied neither you nor me.

Many a friend from bush or burrow
To Riley's hand would run or fly,
And soft he'd sing and sweet he'd whistle
Whatever the weather in the sky.

Till one winter's morning Riley
From the meadow vanished clean.
Gone was the rusty tin, the timber,
As if old Riley had never been.

What strange secret had old Riley?
Where did he come from? Where did he go?
Why was his heart as light as summer?
Never know now, said the jay. *Never know.*

Charles Causley

The Blue Jay

The blue jay with a crest on his head
Comes round the cabin in the snow.
He runs in the snow like a bit of blue metal,
Turning his back on everything.

From the pine-tree that towers and hisses like a pillar of
        shaggy cloud
Immense above the cabin
Comes a strident laugh as we approach, this little black
        dog and I.
So halts the little black bitch on four spread paws in the
        snow
And looks up inquiringly into the pillar of cloud,
With a tinge of misgiving.
Ca-a-a! comes the scrape of ridicule out of the tree.
What voice of the Lord is that, from the tree of smoke?

Oh Bibbles, little black bitch in the snow,
With a pinch of snow in the groove of your silly snub
        nose,
What do you look at *me* for?
What do you look at me for, with such misgiving?

It's the blue jay laughing at us.
It's the blue jay jeering at us, Bibs.

Every day since the snow is here
The blue jay paces round the cabin, very busy, picking up
       bits,
Turning his back on us all,
And bobbing his thick dark crest about the snow, as if
       darkly saying:
I ignore those folk who look out.

You acid-blue metallic bird,
You thick bird with a strong crest
Who are you?
Whose boss are you, with all your bully way?
You copper-sulphate blue-bird!

D. H. Lawrence

'Woodlands winter'

Woodlands winter
where leaves were green:
my red is the rowan
my white the gean.

Seán Rafferty

A Point of View

People who live admist fine scenery are apt to treat it with contempt, partly from familiarity and partly (I think) because they do not see the scenery as other people see it. You form a higher opinion of a man if you have only seen him at his best, than if you have also seen him at his worst and in all intermediate states. It is the same with scenery. Most strangers see this district in the height of summer, whereas the natives see it in the winter time as well, and have both aspects of it in their mind when they are looking at it; and they sometimes show impatience when strangers praise it overmuch. A farmer here was leaning over a gate from which there is a glorious view. Seeing the view, a passer-by remarked to him how glorious it was. The farmer answered, 'Durn the view. I bain't lookin' at no view. I be lookin' how they dratted rabbits 'as ated up my tunnips.'

Cecil Torr

Intercity

Tracks that tie town to town
leave farmland free.
From the tight-stretched train, I see
odd-shaped fields flung down
haphazardly:

in one of which, my eye
is caught
by riderless horse taking a short
canter, on the sly,
like a loose thought.

Christopher Reid

The Cat and the Moon

The cat went here and there
And the moon spun round like a top,
And the nearest kin of the moon,
The creeping cat, looked up.
Black Minnaloushe stared at the moon,
For, wander and wail as he would,
The pure cold light in the sky
Troubled his animal blood.
Minnaloushe runs in the grass
Lifting his delicate feet.
Do you dance, Minnaloushe, do you dance?
When two close kindred meet,
What better than call a dance?
Maybe the moon may learn,
Tired of that courtly fashion,
A new dance turn.
Minnaloushe creeps through the grass
From moonlit place to place,
The sacred moon overhead
Has taken a new phase.
Does Minnaloushe know that his pupils
Will pass from change to change,
And that from round to crescent,
From crescent to round they range?

Minnaloushe creeps through the grass
Alone, important and wise,
And lifts to the changing moon
His changing eyes.

W. B. Yeats

The Gap in the Hedge

That man, Prytherch, with the torn cap,
I saw him often, framed in the gap
Between two hazels with his sharp eyes,
Bright as thorns, watching the sunrise
Filling the valley with its pale yellow
Light, where the sheep and the lambs went haloed
With grey mist lifting from the dew.
Or was it a likeness that the twigs drew
With bold pencilling upon that bare
Piece of the sky? For he's still there
At early morning, when the light is right
And I look up suddenly at a bird's flight.

R. S. Thomas

A Child's Voice

On winter nights shepherd and I
    Down to the lambing shed would go;
Rain round our swinging lamp did fly
    Like shining flakes of snow.

There on a nail our lamp we hung,
    And O it was beyond belief
To see those ewes lick with hot tongues
    The limp wet lambs to life.

A week gone and sun shining warm
    It was as good as gold to hear
Those new-born voices round the farm
    Cry shivering and clear.

Where was a prouder man than I
    Who knew the night those lambs were born
Watching them leap two feet on high
    And stamp the ground in scorn?

Gone sheep and shed and lighted rain
    And blue March morning; yet today
A small voice crying brings again
    Those lambs leaping at play.

Andrew Young

The Comming of Good Luck

So Good-luck came, and on my roofe did light,
Like noyse-lesse Snow; or as the dew of night:
Not all at once, but gently, as the trees
Are, by the Sun-beams, tickel'd by degrees.

Robert Herrick

The Snail

Snailie, snailie, shoot oot yer horn,
An tell me if it will be a bonny day the morn.

Anon (Scottish)

'Another and another and another'

Another and another and another
And still another sunset and sunrise,
The same yet different, different yet the same,
Seen by me now in my declining years
As in my early childhood, youth and manhood;
And by my parents and my parents' parents,
And by the parents of my parents' parents,
And by their parents counted back for ever,
Seen, all their lives long, even as now by me;
And by my children and my children's children
And by the children of my children's children
And by their children counted on for ever
Still to be seen as even now seen by me;
Clear and bright sometimes, sometimes dark and clouded
But still the same sunsetting and sunrise;
The same for ever to the never ending
Line of observers, to the same observer
Through all the changes of his life the same:
Sunsetting and sunrising and sunsetting,
And then again sunrising and sunsetting,
Sunrising and sunsetting evermore.

James Henry

Follower

My father worked with a horse-plough,
His shoulders globed like a full sail strung
Between the shafts and the furrow.
The horses strained at his clicking tongue.

An expert. He would set the wing
And fit the bright steel-pointed sock.
The sod rolled over without breaking.
At the headrig, with a single pluck

Of reins, the sweating team turned round
And back into the land. His eye
Narrowed and angled at the ground,
Mapping the furrow exactly.

I stumbled in his hobnailed wake,
Fell sometimes on the polished sod;
Sometimes he rode me on his back
Dipping and rising to his plod.

I wanted to grow up and plough,
To close one eye, stiffen my arm.
All I ever did was follow
In his broad shadow round the farm.

I was a nuisance, tripping, falling,
Yapping always. But today
It is my father who keeps stumbling
Behind me, and will not go away.

Seamus Heaney

Switch

'Come here,' said Turnbull, 'till you see the sadness
   In the horse's eyes,
If you had such big hooves under you there'd be sadness
   In your eyes too.'

It was clear that he understood so well the sadness
   In the horse's eyes,
And had pondered it so long that in the end he'd plunged
   Into the horse's mind.

I looked at the horse to see the sadness
   Obvious in its eyes,
And saw Turnbull's eyes looking in my direction
   From the horse's head.

I looked at Turnbull one last time
   And saw on his face
Outsize eyes that were dumb with sadness –
   The horse's eyes.

Seán ó Riordáin (Irish, translated by Patrick Crotty)

'Rainbow, rainbow, rin awa hame'

Rainbow, rainbow, rin awa hame;
The coo's tae cauf, the yowe's tae lamb.

Anon (Scottish)

A March Calf

Right from the start he is dressed in his best – his blacks
       and his whites.
Little Fauntleroy – quiffed and glossy,
A Sunday suit, a wedding natty get-up,
Standing in dunged straw

Under cobwebby beams, near the mud wall,
Half of him legs,
Shining-eyed, requiring nothing more
But that mother's milk come back often.

Everything else is in order, just as it is.
Let the summer skies hold off, for the moment.
This is just as he wants it.
A little at a time, of each new thing, is best.

Too much and too sudden is too frightening –
When I block the light, a bulk from space,
To let him in to his mother for a suck,
He bolts a yard or two, then freezes,

Staring from every hair in all directions,
Ready for the worst, shut up in his hopeful religion,
A little syllogism
With a wet blue-reddish muzzle, for God's thumb.

You see all his hopes bustling
As he reaches between the worn rails towards
The top heavy oven of his mother.
He trembles to grow, stretching his curl-tip tongue –

What did cattle ever find here
To make this dear little fellow
So eager to prepare himself?
He is already in the race, and quivering to win –

His new purpled eyeball swivel-jerks
In the elbowing push of his plans.
Hungry people are getting hungrier,
Butchers developing expertise and markets,

But he just wobbles his tail – and glistens
Within his dapper profile
Unaware of how his whole lineage
Has been tied up.

He shivers for feel of the world licking his side.
He is like an ember – one glow
Of lighting himself up
With the fuel of himself, breathing and brightening.

Soon he'll plunge out, to scatter his seething joy,
To be present at the grass,
To be free on the surface of such a wideness,
To find himself himself. To stand. To moo.

Ted Hughes

Song

When icicles hang by the wall
And Dick the shepherd blows his nail,
And Tom bears logs into the hall,
And milk comes frozen home in pail;
When blood is nipt, and ways be foul,
Then nightly sings the staring owl
   Tu-whit!
To-who! A merry note!
While greasy Joan doth keel the pot.

When all about the wind doth blow,
And coughing drowns the parson's saw,
And birds sit brooding in the snow,
And Marian's nose looks red and raw;
When roasted crabs hiss in the bowl—
Then nightly sings the staring owl
    Tu-whit!
To-who! A merry note!
While greasy Joan doth keel the pot.

William Shakespeare

Cock-Crow

Out of the wood of thoughts that grows by night
To be cut down by the sharp axe of light, –
Out of the night, two cocks together crow,
Cleaving the darkness with a silver blow:
And bright before my eyes twin trumpeters stand,
Heralds of splendour, one at either hand,
Each facing each as in a coat of arms:
The milkers lace their boots up at the farms.

Edward Thomas

'I will go with my father a-ploughing'

I will go with my father a-ploughing
To the green field by the sea,
And the rooks and the crows and the sea-gulls
Will come flocking after me.
I will sing to the patient horses,
With the lark in the white of the air,
And my father will sing the plough-song
That blesses the cleaving share.

I will go with my father a-sowing
To the red field by the sea,
And the rooks and the gulls and the starlings
Will come flocking after me.
I will sing to the striding sowers,
With the finch on the greening sloe,
And my father will sing the seed-song
That only the wise men know.

I will go with my father a-reaping
To the brown field by the sea,
And the geese and the crows and the children
Will come flocking after me.
I will sing to the tan-faced reapers,
With the wren in the heat of the sun,
And my father will sing the scythe-song
That joys for the harvest done.

Joseph Campbell

Pied Beauty

Glory be to God for dappled things –
   For skies of couple-colour as a brinded cow;
     For rose-moles all in stipple upon trout that swim;
Fresh-firecoal chestnut-falls; finches' wings;
   Landscape plotted and pieced – fold, fallow, and
                    plough;
   And all trades, their gear and tackle and trim.
All things counter, original, spare, strange;
   Whatever is fickle, freckled (who knows how?)
    With swift, slow; sweet, sour; adazzlc, dim;
He fathers-forth whose beauty is past change:
                Praise him.

Gerard Manley Hopkins

Early Spring

Once more the Heavenly Power
   Makes all things new,
And domes the red-plow'd hills
   With loving blue;
The blackbirds have their wills,
   And throstles too.

Opens a door in Heaven;
   From skies of glass
A Jacob's ladder falls
   On greening grass,
And o'er the mountain-walls
   Young angels pass.

Before them fleets the shower,
   And burst the buds,
And shine the level lands,
   And flash the floods;
The stars are from their hands
   Flung thro' the woods,

The woods with living airs
   How softly fann'd,
Light airs from where the deep,

All down the sand,
Is breathing in his sleep,
Heard by the land.

For now the Heavenly Power
Makes all things new,
And thaws the cold, and fills
The flower with dew;
The blackbirds have their wills
The poets too.

Alfred, Lord Tennyson

Folk Song

The cuckoo she's a pretty bird,
She sings as she flies,
She brings us good tidings,
She tells us no lies;
She sucketh white flowers
For to make her voice clear,
And the more she sings 'cuckoo!'
The summer draws near.

Anon

Answer to a Child's Question

Do you ask what the birds say? The Sparrow, the Dove,
The Linnet and Thrush say, 'I love and I love!'
In the winter they're silent – the wind is so strong;
What it says, I don't know, but it sings a loud song.
But green leaves and blossoms, and sunny warm weather,
And singing, and loving – all come back together.
'I love and I love,' almost all the birds say
From sunrise to star-rise, so gladsome are they!
But the Lark is so brimful of gladness and love,
The green fields below him, the blue sky above,
That he sings, and he sings; and forever sings he –
'I love my Love, and my Love loves me!'
'Tis no wonder that he's full of joy to the brim,
When he loves his Love, and his Love loves him!

Samuel Taylor Coleridge

Hare

He lives on edge throughout his days,
home-fixated, short of sight,
dark heart beating as to burst his breast,
given to sudden panic fright
that sends him hurtling unpredictably
through crops, round quarries, over stones.
And has great eyes, all veined with blood,
and beautifully-articulated bones.

Superstition gives him an unchancy name,
any power that you might mention;
certainly he haunts the corner of the eye,
the edge of the attention
on open downs where movement is surprising,
caught and gone again with every glance,
or jack-knifing quietly through adjacent hedges
beyond the golden stubble-fires' dance.

But he is no more than flesh and blood,
living all his speedy life with fear,
only oblivious of constant danger
at his balletic time of year

when spring skies, winds, the greening furrows
overcome hunger, nervousness, poor sight,
fill him with urgent, huge heroics,
make him stand up and fight.

Molly Holden

From Hereabout Hill

From Hereabout Hill
the sun early rising
looks over his fields
where a river runs by;
at the green of the wheat
and the green of the barley
and Candlelight Meadow
the pride of his eye.

The clock on the wall
strikes eight in the kitchen
the clock in the parlour
says twenty to nine;
the thrush has a song
and the blackbird another
the weather reporter
says cloudless and fine.

It's green by the hedge
and white by the peartree
in Hereabout village
the date is today;

it's seven by the sun
and the time is the springtime
the first of the month and
the month must be May.

Seán Rafferty

Larks

Here I heard the first singing of the birds this year; and I here observed an instance of that *petticoat government*, which, apparently, pervades the whole of animated nature. A lark, very near to me in a ploughed field, rose from the ground, and was saluting the sun with his delightful song. He was got about as high as the dome of St. Paul's, having me for a motionless and admiring auditor, when the hen started up from nearly the same spot whence the cock had risen, flew up and passed close by him. I could not hear what she said; but supposed that she must have given him a pretty smart reprimand; for down she came upon ground, and he, ceasing to sing, took a twirl in the air, and came down after her. Others have, I daresay, seen this a thousand times over; but I never observed it before.

William Cobbett

Nest Eggs

Birds all the sunny day
   Flutter and quarrel
Here in the arbour-like
   Tent of the laurel.

Here in the fork
   The brown nest is seated;
Four little blue eggs
   The mother keeps heated.

While we stand watching her,
   Staring like gabies,
Safe in each egg are the
   Bird's little babies.

Soon the frail eggs they shall
   Chip, and upspringing
Make all the April woods
   Merry with singing.

Younger than we are,
   O children, and frailer,
Soon in blue air they'll be,
   Singer and sailor.

We, so much older,
    Taller and stronger,
We shall look down on the
    Birdies no longer.

They shall go flying
    With musical speeches
High overhead in the
    Tops of the beeches.

In spite of our wisdom
    And sensible talking,
We on our feet must go
    Plodding and walking.

Robert Louis Stevenson

The Marriage of the Frog and the Mouse

It was the frog in the well,
   Humbledum, humbledum,
And the merry mouse in the mill,
    Tweedle, tweedle, twino.

The frog would a-wooing ride
Sword and buckler by his side.

When he upon his high horse set,
His boots they shone as black as jet.

When he came to the merry mill-pin,
'Lady Mouse, been you within?'

Then came out the dusty mouse:
'I am Lady of this house:

Hast thou any mind of me?'
'I have e'en great mind of thee?'

'Who shall this marriage make?'
'Our Lord which is the rat.'

'What shall we have to our supper?'
'Three beans in a pound of butter?'

When supper they were at,
The frog, the mouse, and e'en the rat;

Then came in Gib our cat,
And catched the mouse e'en by the back.

Then did they separate,
And the frog leaped on the floor so flat.

Then came in Dick our drake,
And drew the frog e'en to the lake.

The rat ran up the wall,
    Humbledum, humbledum;
A goodly company, the Devil go with all!
        Tweedle, tweedle twino.

T. Ravenscroft

We Field-Women

How it rained
When we worked at Flintcomb-Ash,
And could not stand upon the hill
Trimming swedes for the slicing-mill.
The wet washed through us – plash, plash, plash:
How it rained!

How it snowed
When we crossed from Flintcomb-Ash
To the Great Barn for drawing reed,
Since we could nowise chop a swede. –
Flakes in each doorway and casement-sash:
How it snowed!

How it shone
When we went from Flintcomb-Ash
To start at dairywork once more
In the laughing meads, with cows three-score,
And pails, and songs, and love – too rash:
How it shone!

Thomas Hardy

Proud Songsters

The thrushes sing as the sun is going,
And the finches whistle in ones and pairs,
And as it gets dark loud nightingales
    In bushes
Pipe, as they can when April wears,
  As if all Time were theirs.

These are brand-new birds of twelve-months' growing,
Which a year ago, or less than twain,
No finches were, nor nightingales,
    Nor thrushes,
But only particles of grain,
  And earth, and air, and rain.

Thomas Hardy

For a Dewdrop

Small shining drop, no lady's ring
Holds so beautiful a thing.
At sun-up in the early air
The sweetness of the world you snare.
Within your little mirror lie
The green grass and the wingèd fly,
The lowest flower, the tallest tree
In your crystal I can see,
Why, in your tiny globe you hold
The sun himself, a midge of gold!
It makes me wonder if the world
In which so many things are curled,
The world which all men real call,
Is not the real world at all,
But just a drop of dew instead
Swinging on a spider's thread.

Eleanor Farjeon

Cynddylan on a Tractor

Ah, you should see Cynddylan on a tractor.
Gone the old look that yoked him to the soil;
He's a new man now, part of the machine,
His nerves of metal and his blood oil.
The clutch curses, but the gears obey
His least bidding, and lo, he's away
Out of the farmyard, scattering hens.
Riding to work now as a great man should,
He is the knight at arms breaking the fields'
Mirror of silence, emptying the wood
Of foxes and squirrels and bright jays.
The sun comes over the tall trees
Kindling all the hedges, but not for him
Who runs his engine on a different fuel.
And all the birds are singing, bills wide in vain,
As Cynddylan passes proudly up the lane.

R. S. Thomas

Hedgehog

The snail moves like a
Hovercraft, held up by a
Rubber cushion of itself,
Sharing its secret

With the hedgehog. The hedgehog
Shares its secret with no one.
We say, Hedgehog, come out
Of yourself and we will love you.

We mean no harm. We want
Only to listen to what
You have to say. We want
Your answers to our questions.

The hedgehog gives nothing
Away, keeping itself to itself.
We wonder what a hedgehog
Has to hide, why it so distrusts.

We forget the god
Under this crown of thorns.
We forget that never again
Will a god trust in the world.

Paul Muldoon

No Newspapers

Where, to me, is the loss
    Of the scenes they saw – of the sounds they heard;
A butterfly flits across,
    Or a bird;
The moss is growing on the wall,
    I heard the leaf of the poppy fall.

Mary E. Coleridge

Hearts-Ease

There is a flower I wish to wear,
  But not until first worne by you . . .
Hearts-ease . . . of all Earth's flowers most rare;
  Bring it; and bring enough for two.

Walter Savage Landor

'Four seeds in a hole'

Four seeds in a hole:
One for the rook, and one for the crow;
And one to rot, and one to grow.

or

Four seeds in a hole:
One for the buds,
One for the meece,
And two for Maaster.

Anon

'Cadows and crows'

Cadows and crows,
Take care of your toes.
For here come my clappers
To knock you down back'uds.
Holla ca-whoo! Ca-whoo!

Here come a stone
To break your back-bone:
Here come the farmer with his big gun
And you must fly and I must run.
Holla ca-whoo! Ca-whoo!

Anon

A Crow and a Scarecrow

A crow and a scarecrow fell in love
out in the fields.
The scarecrow's heart was a stuffed leather glove
but his love was real.
The crow perched on the stick of a wrist
and opened her beak:
Scarecrow, I love you madly, deeply.
Speak.

Crow, rasped the Scarecrow, *hear these words*
from my straw throat.
I love you too
from my boot to my hat
by way of my old tweed coat.
Croak.
The crow crowed back,
Scarecrow, let me take you away
to live in a tall tree.
I'll be a true crow wife to you
if you'll marry me.

The Scarecrow considered.
Crow, tell me how
a groom with a broomstick spine

can take a bride.
I know you believe in love
in these button eyes
but I'm straw inside
and straw can't fly.

The crow pecked at his heart
with her beak
then flapped away,
and back and forth she flew to him
all day, all day,
until she pulled one last straw
from his tattered vest
and soared across the sun with it
to her new nest.

And there she slept, high in her tree,
winged, in a bed of love.
Night fell.
The slow moon rose
over a meadow,
a heap of clothes,
   two boots,
   an empty glove.

Carol Ann Duffy

64

The Hawk

On Sunday the hawk fell on Bigging
    And a chicken screamed
    Lost in its own little snowstorm.
And on Monday he fell on the moor
    And the Field Club
    Raised a hundred silent prisms.
And on Tuesday he fell on the hill
    And the happy lamb
    Never knew why the loud collie straddled him.
And on Wednesday he fell on a bush
    And the blackbird
    Laid by his little flute for the last time.
And on Thursday he fell on Cleat
    And peerie Tom's rabbit
    Swung in a single arc from shore to hill.
And on Friday he fell on a ditch
    But the questing cat,
    That rival, rampant, fluttered his flame.
And on Saturday he fell on Bigging
    And Jock lowered his gun
    And nailed a small wing over the corn.

George Mackay Brown

The Whipper-In

'My father was the whipper-in, –
    Is still – if I'm not misled?
And now I see, where the hedge is thin,
    A little spot of red;
    Surely it is my father
    Going to the kennel-shed!

'I cursed and fought my father – aye,
    And sailed to a foreign land;
And feeling sorry, I'm back, to stay,
    Please God, as his helping hand.
    Surely it is my father
    Near where the kennels stand?'

'– True. Whipper-in he used to be
    For twenty years or more;
And you did go away to sea
    As youths have done before.
    Yes, oddly enough that red there
    Is the very coat he wore.

'But he – he's dead; was thrown somehow,
    And gave his back a crick,
And though that is his coat, 'tis now

The scarecrow of a rick;
You'll see when you get nearer –
'Tis spread out on a stick.

'You see, when all had settled down
Your mother's things were sold,
And she went back to her own town,
And the coat, ate out with mould,
Is now used by the farmer
For scaring, as 'tis old.'

Thomas Hardy

Nuts in May

Here we come gathering nuts in May,
   Nuts in May, nuts in May,
Here we come gathering nuts in May
   On a cold and frosty morning.

Who will you have for nuts in May,
   Nuts in May, nuts in May,
Who will you have for nuts in May
   On a cold and frosty morning?

Anon

This Little Pig

This little pig went to markct;
This little pig stayed at home;
This little pig had roast beef;
This little pig had none;
And this little pig cried, Wee-wec-wce!
   All the way home.

Anon

Old Shepherd's Prayer

Up to the bed by the window, where I be lyin',
Comes bells and bleat of the flock, wi' they two
        children's clack.
Over, from under the eaves there's the starlings flyin',
And down in yard, fit to burst his chain,
        yapping out at Sue I do hear young Mac.

Turning around like a falled-over sack
I can see team ploughin' in Whithy-bush field and
        meal carts startin' up road to Church-Town;
Saturday arternoon the men goin' back
And the women from market, trapin' home over the down.

Heavenly Master, I wud like to wake to they same green
        places
Where I know'd for breakin' dogs and follerin' sheep.
And if I may not walk in th' old ways and look on th' old
        faces
I wud sooner sleep.

Charlotte Mew

Baa Baa Black Sheep

Baa, baa, black sheep,
  Have you any wool?
Yes, sir, yes, sir,
  Three bags full;
One for the master,
  And one for the dame,
And one for the little boy
  Who lives down the lane.

Anon

Weasels at Work

Every creature in its own way
Mistakes the weasel
For somebody else – too late.

The weasel's white chest
Is the dainty pinafore of the waitress
Who brings the field-vole knife and fork.

The weasel's black ripe eyes
Brim with a heady elderberry wine
That makes the rat drunk.

The weasel's fully-fashioned coat,
Lion-colour, wins her admittance
To the club of snobby goslings.

When the weasel dances her belly dance
Brainless young buck rabbits
Simpering, go weak at the knees.

When the weasel laughs
Even the mole sees the joke
And rolls in the aisles, helpless.

*

His face is a furry lizard's face, but prettier.

Only the weasel
Is wick as a weasel.
Whipping whisk

Of a grim cook. And a lit trail
Of gunpowder, he fizzes
Towards a shocking stop.

His tail jaunts along for the laughs.

His grandfather, to keep him active,
Buried the family jewels

Under some rabbit's ear.

Tyrannosaur – miniaturised
To slip through every loop-hole
In the laws of rats and mice.

Terrorist
Of the eggs –

Over the rim of the thrush's nest
The weasel's face, bright as the evening star,
Brings night.

Ted Hughes

Sheep Shearing, Skye

I park outside the pen.
They are all jostling and shoving
panicking really panicking; the fear,
I can smell it stronger than ferns
or seaweed. *On you go before me*
That's what it's like. Really pushing
each other about. Out for themselves.

You point at the old man with the bunnet,
and the young one with his floppy curls—
I could see them cut. The whole lot. See how
he'd like it. Let me try that on you son.
They each take one: hooves on tiptoe.
Neck way back. Arms round like a noose.
That high strangled sound; *save me.*

My wee boy cries like a lamb. Can't stand it.
The constant clip clip clip and all that wool
falling to the ground, falling like snow. Years ago
I remember my dad saved one from barbed wire.
Its hind legs' strong frantic kick when it ran off.
I walk on down the road; bracken on one side
the sea below the other. The buggy gets caught

In a cattle grid. You laugh. I'm caught
too. And the midges will be out soon.
I've got no lavender to keep them off.
But nothing beats them anyway. It's whole gangs
of them you have to deal with. And, suddenly;
most of them are done. All bald and spindly.
Fragile like another animal was hiding underneath

All that time, like a convict. Look. Look.
You point at the barenaked creatures.
All their loot lying on the ground. Look.
Yes, it will grow back, honest it will.
Though right now, it is unimaginable.
The old man and the young one wave hello.
'Whose they' you say. 'Whose those men?'

Jackie Kay

From Dart

listen,
a
lark
spinning
around
one
note
splitting
and
mending
it

Alice Oswald

Laughing Song

When the green woods laugh with the voice of joy,
And the dimpling stream runs laughing by;
When the air does laugh with our merry wit,
And the green hill laughs with the noise of it;

When the meadows laugh with lively green,
And the grasshopper laughs in the merry scene;
When Mary and Susan and Emily
With their sweet round mouths sing 'Ha, Ha, He!'

When the painted birds laugh in the shade,
Where our table with cherries and nuts is spread:
Come live, and be merry, and join with me,
To sing the sweet chorus of 'Ha, Ha, He!'

William Blake

'There is wild wood'

There is Wild wood,
A Mild hood
To the sheep on the lea o' the down,
Where the golden furze,
With its green, thin spurs,
Doth catch at the maiden's gown.

John Keats

'And O, and O'

And O, and O
The daisies blow
And the primroses are waken'd,
And violets white
Sit in silver plight,
And the green bud's as long as the spike end.

John Keats

The Huntsmen

Three jolly gentlemen,
  In coats of red,
Rode their horses
  Up to bed.

Three jolly gentlemen
  Snored till morn,
Their horses champing
  The golden corn.

Three jolly gentlemen,
  At break of day,
Came clitter-clatter down the stairs
  And galloped away.

Walter de la Mare

A Scherzo. (A Shy Person's Wishes)

With the wasp at the innermost heart of a peach,
On a sunny wall out of tip-toe reach,
With the trout in the darkest summer pool,
With the fern-seed clinging behind its cool
Smooth frond, in the chink of an aged tree,
In the woodbine's horn with the drunken bee,
With the mouse in its nest in a furrow old,
With the chrysalis wrapt in its gauzy fold;
With things that are hidden, and safe, and bold,
With things that are timid, and shy, and free,
Wishing to be;
With the nut in its shell, with the seed in its pod,
With the corn as it sprouts in the kindly clod,
Far down where the secret of beauty shows
In the bulb of the tulip, before it blows;
With things that are rooted, and firm, and deep,
Quiet to lie, and dreamless to sleep;
With things that are chainless, and tameless, and proud,
With the fire in the jagged thunder-cloud,
With the wind in its sleep, with the wind in its waking,
With the drops that go to the rainbow's making,
Wishing to be with the light leaves shaking,
Or stones on some desolate highway breaking;
Far up on the hills, where no foot surprises

The dew as it falls, or the dust as it rises;
To be couched with the beast in its torrid lair,
Or drifting on ice with the polar bear,
With the weaver at work at his quiet loom;
Anywhere, anywhere, out of this room!

Dora Greenwell

Fetching Cows

The black one, last as usual, swings her head
And coils a black tongue round a grass-tuft. I
Watch her soft weight come down, her split feet spread.

In front, the others swing and slouch; they roll
Their great Greek eyes and breathe out milky gusts
From muzzles black and shiny as wet coal.

The collie trots, bored, at my heels, then plops
Into the ditch. The sea makes a tired sound
That's always stopping though it never stops.

A haycart squats prickeared against the sky.
Hay breath and milk breath. Far out in the West
The wrecked sun founders though its colours fly.

The collie's bored. There's nothing to control . . .
The black cow is two native carriers
Bringing its belly home, slung from a pole.

Norman MacCaig

Wagtail and Baby

A baby watched a ford, whereto
    A wagtail came for drinking;
A blaring bull went wading through,
    The wagtail showed no shrinking.

A stallion splashed his way across,
    The birdie nearly sinking;
He gave his plumes a twitch and toss,
    And held his own unblinking.

Next saw the baby round the spot
    A mongrel slowly slinking:
The wagtail gazed, but faltered not
    In dip and sip and prinking.

A perfect gentlemen then neared;
    The wagtail, in a winking,
With terror rose and disappeared;
    The baby fell a-thinking.

Thomas Hardy

'Thistles cut in May'

Thistles cut in May
Come again next day.
Thistles cut in June
Come up again soon.
Cut them in July,
They'll be sure to die.

Anon

John Barleycorn

There came three men from out the West
    Their victory to try;
And they have taken a solemn oath
    John Barleycorn should die.

They took a plough and ploughed him in,
    Laid clods upon his head,
And they have taken a solemn oath
    John Barleycorn is dead.

So there he lay for a full fortnight,
    Till the dew from heaven did fall:
John Barleycorn sprang up again,
    And sore surprised them all.

But when he faced the summer sun,
    He looked both pale and wan –
For all he had a spiky beard
    To show he was a man.

But soon came men with sickles sharp
    And shopped him to the knee.
They rolled and tied him by the waist,
    And served him barbarously.

With forks they stuck him to the heart
    And banged him over stones,
And sent the men with holly clubs
    To batter at his bones.

But Barleycorn has noble blood:
    It lives when it is shed:
It fills the cupboard and the purse
    With gold and meat and bread.

O Barleycorn is the choicest grain
    That e'er was sown on land:
It will do more than any grain
    By the turning of your hand.

Anon

The Mower to the Glo-Worms

Ye living Lamps, by whose dear light
The Nightingale does sit so late,
And studying all the Summer-night,
Her matchless Songs does meditate;

Ye Country Comets, that portend
No War, nor Princes funeral,
Shining unto no higher end
Than to presage the Grasses fall;

Ye Glo-worms, whose officious Flame
To wandring Mowers shows the way,
That in the Night have lost their aim,
And after foolish Fires do stray;

Your courteous Lights in vain you waste,
Since *Juliana* here is come,
For She my Mind hath so displac'd
That I shall never find my home.

Andrew Marvell

In a Cornfield

A silence of full noontide heat
Grew on them at their toil:
The farmer's dog woke up from sleep,
The green snake hid her coil
Where grass grew thickest; bird and beast
Sought shadows as they could,
The reaping men and women paused
And sat down where they stood;
They ate and drank and were refreshed,
For rest from toil is good.

Christina Rossetti

Mouse's Nest

I found a ball of grass among the hay
And proged it as I passed and went away
And when I looked I fancied somthing stirred
And turned agen and hoped to catch the bird
When out an old mouse bolted in the wheat
With all her young ones hanging at her teats
She looked so odd and so grotesque to me
I ran and wondered what the thing could be
And pushed the knapweed bunches where I stood
When the mouse hurried from the crawling brood
The young ones squeaked and when I went away
She found her nest again among the hay
The water o'er the pebbles scarce could run
And broad old cesspools glittered in the sun

John Clare

'What could be lovelier than to hear'

What could be lovelier than to hear
The summer rain
Cutting across the heat, as scythes
Cut across grain?
Falling upon the steaming roof
With sweet uproar,
Tapping and rapping wildly
At the door?

No, do not lift the latch,
But through the pane
We'll stand and watch the circus pageant
Of the rain,
And see the lightning, like a tiger,
Striped and dread,
And hear the thunder cross the sky
With elephant tread.

Elizabeth Coatsworth

The Snare

I hear a sudden cry of pain!
There is a rabbit in a snare:
Now I hear the cry again,
But I cannot tell from where.

But I cannot tell from where
He is calling out for aid!
Crying on the frightened air,
Making everything afraid!

Making everything afraid,
Wrinkling up his little face!
As he cries again for aid;
– And I cannot find the place!

And I cannot find the place
Where his paw is in the snare!
Little One! Oh, Little One!
I am searching everywhere!

James Stephens

Hay-making

You know the hay's in
when gates hang slack
in the lanes. These hot nights
the fallen fields lie open
under the moon's clean sheets.

The homebound road is
sweet with the liquors
of the grasses, air
green with the pastels
of stirred hayfields.

Down at Fron Felen
in the loaded barn
new bales displace
stale darknesses. Breathe.
Remember finding
first kittens, first love
in the scratch of the hay,
our sandals filled with seeds.

Gillian Clarke

The Rewards of Farming

Let the Wealthy and Great,
Roll in Splendour and State,
I envy them not, I declare it;
I eat my own Lamb,
My Chickens and Ham,
I shear my own Fleece and I wear it.
I have Lawns, I have Bow'rs,
I have Fruits, I have Flowers,
The Lark is my morning alarmer;
　　So jolly Boys now,
Here's God speed the Plough,
　　Long Life and Success to the Farmer!

Anon

The Hayloft

Through all the pleasant meadow-side
    The grass grew shoulder-high,
Till the shining scythes went far and wide
    And cut it down to dry.

These green and sweetly smelling crops
    They led in waggons home;
And they piled them here in mountain tops
    For mountaineers to roam.

Here is Mount Clear, Mount Rusty-Nail,
    Mount Eagle and Mount High; –
The mice that in these mountains dwell,
    No happier are than I!

O what a joy to clamber there,
    O what a place for play,
With the sweet, the dim, the dusty air,
    The happy hills of hay!

Robert Louis Stevenson

Summer Farm

Straws like tame lightnings lie about the grass
And hang zigzag on hedges. Green as glass
The water in the horse-trough shines.
Nine ducks go wobbling by in two straight lines.

A hen stares at nothing with one eye,
Then picks it up. Out of an empty sky
A swallow falls and, flickering through
The barn, dives up again into the dizzy blue.

I lie, not thinking, in the cool, soft grass,
Afraid of where a thought might take me – as
This grasshopper with plated face
Unfolds his legs and finds himself in space.

Self under self, a pile of selves I stand
Threaded on time, and with metaphysic hand
Lift the farm like a lid and see
Farm within farm, and in the centre, me.

Norman MacCaig

Lavender's Blue

Lavender's blue, dilly, dilly, lavender's green,
When I am king, dilly, dilly, you shall be queen;
Call up your men, dilly, dilly, set them to work,
Some to the plough, dilly, dilly, some to the cart;
Some to make hay dilly, dilly, some to thresh corn;
Whilst you and I, dilly, dilly, keep ourselves warm.

Anon

Peacock

I see you there, cool as a cucumber
you see me, working hard in the summer
with your tail like a fan of colour
which no doubt you are proud to wear
but I wish you would share it
and give me a waft of fresh air.

A young writer who came and spent a week at
Wick Court, a Farm for City Children

Writing in Prison

Years ago I was a gardener.
I grew the flowers of my childhood,
lavender and wayside lilies
and my first love the cornflower.

The wind on the summer wheat.
The blue glaze in the vanished woods.
In the space of my yard I glimpsed again
all the lost places of my life.

I was remaking them. Here in a space
smaller still I make them again.

Ken Smith

The Babes in the Wood

My dear, do you know
How a long time ago,
    Two poor little children,
Whose names I don't know,
Were stolen away
On a fine summer's day,
    And left in a wood,
As I've heard people say.

And when it was night,
So sad was their plight,
    The sun it went down,
And the moon gave no light!
They sobbed and they sighed,
And they bitterly cried,
    And the poor little things,
They lay down and died.

And when they were dead,
The robins so red
    Brought strawberry leaves
And over them spread;

And all the day long,
They sang them this song –
    Poor babes in the wood!
    Poor babes in the wood!
And won't you remember
    The babes in the wood?

Anon

Childhood among the Ferns

I sat one sprinkling day upon the lea,
Where tall-stemmed ferns spread out luxuriantly,
And nothing but those tall ferns sheltered me.

The rain gained strength, and damped each lopping
        frond,
Ran down their stalks beside me and beyond,
And shaped slow-creeping rivulets as I conned,

With pride, my spray-roofed house. And though anon
Some drops pierced its green rafters, I sat on,
Making pretence I was not rained upon.

The sun then burst, and brought forth a sweet breath
From the limp ferns as they dried underneath:
I said: 'I could live on here thus till death;'

And queried in the green rays as I sate:
'Why should I have to grow to man's estate,
And this afar-noised World perambulate?'

Thomas Hardy

Up on the Moors with Keeper

Three girls under the sun's rare brilliance
out on the moors, hitching their skirts
over bog-myrtle and bilberry.

They've kicked up their heels at a dull brother
whose *keep still can't you?* wants to fix
them to canvas. Emily's dog stares at these

three girls under the juggling larks
pausing to catch that song on a hesitant wind,
all wings and faces dipped in light.

What could there be to match this glory?
High summer, a scent of absent rain,
away from the dark house, father and duty.

Maura Dooley

Net and River

The old bus, nose to the road like a dog,
takes them all the way to the village
with its one shop and shining river.

The net she picks is green, uncertain
on its skinny pole as she dips it
back and forth, between the weeds,
over the stones and catches a fish.

A fish. A flicker and jump in water,
in air: a flash like memory itself.

Watching its ugly gasp for life,
the river fall from its back in tears,
the unkind swat of its head on stone,
she has to drop it back again

and let the waters close, the ripples spread
wide and wider till they can't be seen,
till the lip of deepest water stops its trembling.

Maura Dooley

The River God

I may be smelly and I may be old,
Rough in my pebbles, reedy in my pools,
But where my fish float by I bless their swimming
And I like the people to bathe in me, especially women.
But I can drown the fools
Who bathe too close to the weir, contrary to rules.
And they take a long time drowning
As I throw them up now and then in a spirit of clowning.
Hi yih, yippity-yap, merrily I flow.
O I may be an old foul river but I have plenty of go.
Once there was a lady who was too bold
She bathed in me by the tall black cliff where the water
       runs cold.
So I brought her down here
To be my beautiful dear.
Oh will she stay with me will she stay
This beautiful lady, or will she go away?
She lies in my beautiful deep river bed with many a weed
To hold her, and many a waving reed.
Oh who would guess what a beautiful white face lies there
Waiting for me to smooth and wash away the fear
She looks at me with. Hi yih, do not let her

Go. There is no one on earth who does not forget her
Now. They say I am a foolish old smelly river
But they do not know of my wide original bed
Where the lady waits, with her golden sleepy head.
If she wishes to go I will not forgive her.

Stevie Smith

'The careful angler'

The careful angler chose his nook
At morning by the lilied brook,
And all the noon his rod he plied
By that romantic riverside.
Soon as the evening hours decline
Tranquilly he'll return to dine,
And breathing forth a pious wish,
Will cram his belly full of fish.

Robert Louis Stevenson

A Lake

                A lake
Is a river curled and asleep like a snake.

Thomas Lovell Beddoes

The Lake Isle of Innisfree

I will arise and go now, and go to Innisfree,
And a small cabin build there, of clay and wattles made:
Nine bean-rows will I have there, a hive for the honey-bee,
And live alone in the bee-loud glade.

And I shall have some peace there, for peace comes
        dropping slow,
Dropping from the veils of the morning to where the
        cricket sings;
There midnight's all a glimmer, and noon a purple glow,
And evening full of the linnet's wings.

I will arise and go now, for always night and day
I hear lake water lapping with low sounds by the shore;
While I stand on the roadway, or on the pavements grey,
I hear it in the deep heart's core.

W. B. Yeats

Autumn

A touch of cold in the Autumn night –
I walked abroad,
And saw the ruddy moon lean over a hedge
Like a red-faced farmer.
I did not stop to speak, but nodded,
And round about were the wistful stars
With white faces like town children.

T. E. Hulme

Charm

The owl is abroad, the bat, and the toad,
    And so is the cat-a-mountayne,
The ant, and the mole sit both in a hole,
    And frog peeps out o'the fountayne;
The dogs, they do bay, and the timbrels play,
    The spindle is now a turning;
The moon it is red, and the stars are fled,
    But all the sky is a burning:

Ben Jonson

From Sweeney's Flight

Every night I glean and raid
and comb the floor of the oak wood.
My hands work into leaf and rind,
old roots, old windfalls on the ground,

they rake through matted watercress
and grope among the bog-berries,
cool brooklime, sorrel and damp moss,
wild garlic and wild raspberries,

apples, hazelnuts and acorns,
the haws of sharp, jaggy hawthorns,
the blackberries, the floating weed,
the whole store of the oak wood.

Seamus Heancy

'Pit yer finger in the corbie's hole'

Pit yer finger in the corbie's hole,
The corbie's no at hame;
The corbie's at the back-door,
Pykin at a bane.

Anon (Scottish)

Lord Randal

'O where hae ye been, Lord Randal, my son?
O where hae ye been, my handsome young man?'
'I have been to the wild wood; Mother, make my bed
        soon,
For I'm weary wi hunting, and fain wald lie down.'

'Where gat ye your dinner, Lord Randal, my son?
Where gat ye your dinner, my handsome young man?'
'I dined wi my true-love; Mother, make my bed soon,
For I'm weary wi hunting, and fain wald lie down.'

'What gat ye to your dinner, Lord Randal, my son?
What gat ye to your dinner, my handsome young man?'
'I gat a dish o' wee fishes; Mother, make my bed soon,
For I'm weary wi hunting, and fain wald lie down.'

'What like were the fishes, Lord Randal, my son?
What like were the fishes, my handsome young man?'
'Black-backs and spreckle bellies; Mother, make my bed
        soon,
For I'm weary wi hunting, and fain wald lie down.'

'What became of your bloodhounds, Lord Randal,
        my son?
What became of your bloodhounds, my handsome young
        man?'
'Oh they swelld and they died; Mother, make my bed
        soon,
For I'm weary wi hunting, and fain wald lie down.'

'O I fear ye are poisond, Lord Randal, my son!
O I fear ye are poisond, my handsome young man!'
'O yes! I am poisond; Mother, make my bed soon,
For I'm sick at the heart and I fain wald lie down.'

Anon (Scottish)

The Rat

Strange that you let me come so near
    And send no questing senses out
From eye's dull jelly, shell-pink ear,
    Fierce-whiskered snout.

But clay has hardened in these claws
    And gypsy-like I read too late
In lines scored on your naked paws
    A starry fate.

Even that snake, your tail, hangs dead,
    And as I leave you stiff and still
A death-like quietness has spread
    Across the hill.

Andrew Young

Fern Hill

Now as I was young and easy under the apple boughs
About the lilting house and happy as the grass was green,
  The night above the dingle starry,
    Time let me hail and climb
  Golden in the heydays of his eyes,
And honoured among wagons I was prince of the apple
        towns
And once below a time I lordly had the trees and leaves
    Trail with daisies and barley
  Down the rivers of the windfall light.

And as I was green and carefree, famous among the barns
About the happy yard and singing as the farm was home,
  In the sun that is young once only,
    Time let me play and be
  Golden in the mercy of his means,
And green and golden I was huntsman and herdsman, the
        calves
Sang to my horn, the foxes on the hills barked clear and
        cold,
    And the sabbath rang slowly
  In the pebbles of the holy streams.

All the sun long it was running, it was lovely, the hay
Fields high as the house, the tunes from the chimneys, it
was air
And playing, lovely and watery
And fire green as grass.
And nightly under the simple stars
As I rode to sleep the owls were bearing the farm away,
All the moon long I heard, blessed among stables, the
nightjars
Flying with the ricks, and the horses
Flashing into the dark.

And then to awake, and the farm, like a wanderer white
With the dew, come back, the cock on his shoulder: it
was all
Shining, it was Adam and maiden,
The sky gathered again
And the sun grew round that very day.
So it must have been after the birth of the simple light
In the first, spinning place, the spellbound horses walking
warm
Out of the whinnying green stable
On to the fields of praise.

And honoured among foxes and pheasants by the gay
      house
Under the new made clouds and happy as the heart was
      long,
  In the sun born over and over,
   I ran my heedless ways,
  My wishes raced through the house high hay
And nothing I cared, at my sky blue trades, that time
      allows
In all his tuneful turning so few and such morning songs
  Before the children green and golden
   Follow him out of grace,

Nothing I cared, in the lamb white days, that time would
      take me
Up to the swallow thronged loft by the shadow of my
      hand,
  In the moon that is always rising,
   Nor that riding to sleep
  I should hear him fly with the high fields
And wake to the farm forever fled from the childless land.
Oh as I was young and easy in the mercy of his means,
   Time held me green and dying
  Though I sang in my chains like the sea.

Dylan Thomas

On the Grasshopper and Cricket

The poetry of earth is never dead:
  When all the birds are faint with the hot sun,
  And hide in cooling trees, a voice will run
From hedge to hedge about the new-mown mead;
That is the Grasshopper's – he takes the lead
  In summer luxury, – he has never done
  With his delights; for when tired out with fun
He rests at ease beneath some pleasant weed.
The poetry of earth is ceasing never:
  On a lone winter evening, when the frost
  Has wrought a silence, from the stove there shrills
The Cricket's song, in warmth increasing ever,
  And seems to one in drowsiness half lost,
  The Grasshopper's among some grassy hills.

John Keats

Aspens

All day and night, save winter, every weather,
Above the inn, the smithy, and the shop,
The aspens at the cross-roads talk together
Of rain, until their last leaves fall from the top.

Out of the blacksmith's cavern comes the ringing
Of hammer, shoe, and anvil; out of the inn
The clink, the hum, the roar, the random singing –
The sounds that for these fifty years have been.

The whisper of the aspens is not drowned,
And over lightless pane and footless road,
Empty as sky, with every other sound
Not ceasing, calls their ghosts from their abode,

A silent smithy, a silent inn, nor fails
In the bare moonlight or the thick-furred gloom,
In tempest or the night of nightingales,
To turn the cross-roads to a ghostly room.

And it would be the same were no house near.
Over all sorts of weather, men, and times,
Aspens must shake their leaves and men may hear
But need not listen, more than to my rhymes.

Whatever wind blows, while they and I have leaves
We cannot other than an aspen be
That ceaselessly, unreasonably grieves,
Or so men think who like a different tree.

Edward Thomas

Song

A widow bird sate mourning for her love
   Upon a wintry bough;
The frozen wind crept on above,
   The freezing stream below.

There was no leaf upon the forest bare,
   No flower upon the ground,
And little motion in the air
   Except the mill-wheel's sound.

Percy Bysshe Shelley

The Miller's Song

There was a jolly miller once,
Lived on the river Dee;
He worked and sang from morn till night,
No lark more blithe than he.
And this the burden of his song
Forever used to be,
I care for nobody, no not I,
If nobody cares for me.

Anon

The Sands of Dee

'O Mary, go and call the cattle home,
　　And call the cattle home,
　　And call the cattle home
　Across the sands of Dee;'
The western wind was wild and dank with foam,
　And all alone went she.

The western tide crept up along the sand,
　　And o'er and o'er the sand,
　　And round and round the sand,
　As far as eye could see.
The rolling mist came down and hid the land:
　And never home came she.

'Oh! is it weed, or fish, or floating hair –
　　A tress of golden hair,
　　A drownèd maiden's hair
　Above the nets at sea?
Was never salmon yet that shone so fair
　Among the stakes on Dee.'

They rowed her in across the rolling foam,
     The cruel crawling foam,
     The cruel hungry foam,
   To her grave beside the sea:
But still the boatmen hear her call the cattle home
   Across the sands of Dee.

Charles Kingsley

Perfect

On the Western Seaboard of South Uist

Los muertos abren los ojos a los que viven

I found a pigeon's skull on the machair,
All the bones pure white and dry, and chalky,
But perfect,
Without a crack or a flaw anywhere.

At the back, rising out of the beak,
Were domes like bubbles of thin bone,
Almost transparent, where the brain had been
That fixed the tilt of the wings.

Hugh MacDiarmid

New Foal

Yesterday he was nowhere to be found
In the skies or under the skies.

Suddenly he's here – a warm heap
Of ashes and embers, fondled by small draughts.

A star dived from outer space – flared
And burned out in the straw.
Now something is stirring in the smoulder.
We call it a foal.

Still stunned
He has no idea where he is.
His eyes, dew-dusky, explore gloom walls and a glare
        doorspace.
Is this the world?
It puzzles him. It is a great numbness.

He pulls himself together, getting used to the weight of
        things
And to that tall horse nudging him, and to this straw.

He rests
From the first blank shock of light, the empty daze

Of the questions –
What has happened? What am I?

His ears keep on asking, gingerly.

But his legs are impatient,
Recovering from so long being nothing
They are restless with ideas, they start to try a few out,
Angling this way and that,
Feeling for leverage, learning fast –

And suddenly he's up

And stretching – a giant hand
Strokes him from nose to heel
Perfecting his outline, as he tightens
The knot of himself.
                                    Now he comes teetering
Over the weird earth. His nose
Downy and magnetic, draws him, incredulous,
Towards his mother. And the world is warm
And careful and gentle. Touch by touch
Everything fits him together.

Soon he'll be almost a horse.
He wants only to be Horse,

Pretending each day more and more Horse
Till hc's perfect Horse. Then unearthly Horse
Will surge through him, weightless, a spinning of flame
Under sudden gusts,

It will coil his eyeball and his heel
In a single terror – like the awe
Between lightning and thunderclap.

And curve his neck, like a sea-monster emerging
Among foam,

And fling the new moons through his stormy banner,
And the full moons and the dark moons.

Ted Hughes

Digging

Today I think
Only with scents, – scents dead leaves yield,
And bracken, and wild carrot's seed,
And the square mustard field;

Odours that rise
When the spade wounds the root of tree,
Rose, currant, raspberry, or goutweed,
Rhubarb or celery:

The smoke's smell, too,
Flowing from where a bonfire burns
The dead, the waste, the dangerous,
And all to sweetness turns.

It is enough
To smell, to crumble the dark earth,
While the robin sings over again
Sad songs of Autumn mirth.

Edward Thomas

Autumn Ploughing

After the ranks of stubble have lain bare,
And field mice and the finches' beaks have found
The last spilled seed corn left upon the ground;
And no more swallows miracle in air;

When the green tuft no longer hides the hare,
And dropping starling flights at evening come;
When birds, except the robin, have gone dumb,
And leaves are rustling downwards everywhere;

Then out, with the great horses, come the ploughs,
And all day long the slow procession goes,
Darkening the stubble fields with broadening strips.

Gray sea-gulls settle after to carouse:
Harvest prepares upon the harvest's close,
Before the blackbird pecks the scarlet hips.

John Masefield

The Hill Farmer Speaks

I am the farmer, stripped of love
And thought and grace by the land's hardness:
But what I am saying over the fields'
Desolate acres, rough with dew,
Is, Listen, listen, I am a man like you.

The wind goes over the hill pastures
Year after year, and the ewes starve,
Milkless, for want of the new grass.
And I starve, too, for something the spring
Can never foster in veins run dry.

The pig is a friend, the cattle's breath
Mingles with mine in the still lanes;
I wear it willingly like a cloak
To shelter me from your curious gaze.

The hens go in and out at the door
From sun to shadow, as stray thoughts pass
Over the floor of my wide skull.
The dirt is under my cracked nails;
The tale of my life is smirched with dung;
The phlegm rattles. But what I am saying
Over the grasses rough with dew
Is, Listen, listen, I am a man like you.

R. S. Thomas

'When the wind is in the east'

When the wind is in the east
tis good for neither man nor beast
when the wind is in the south
it is in the rain's mouth

Anon

The Way Through the Woods

They shut the road through the woods
Seventy years ago.
Weather and rain have undone it again,
And now you would never know
There was once a road through the woods
Before they planted the trees.
It is underneath the coppice and heath,
And the thin anemones.
Only the keeper sees
That, where the ring-dove broods,
And the badgers roll at ease,
There was once a road through the woods.

Yet, if you enter the woods
Of a summer evening late,
When the night-air cools on the trout-ringed pool
Where the otter whistles his mate,
(They fear not men in the woods,
Because they see so few.)

You will hear the beat of a horse's feet,
And the swish of a skirt in the dew,
Steadily cantering through
The misty solitudes,
As though they perfectly knew
The old lost road through the woods . . .
But there is no road through the woods.

Rudyard Kipling

Out in the Dark

Out in the dark over the snow
The fallow fawns invisible go
With the fallow doe;
And the winds blow
Fast as the stars are slow.

Stealthily the dark haunts round
And, when the lamp goes, without sound
At a swifter bound
Than the swiftest hound,
Arrives, and all else is drowned;

And star and I and wind and deer,
Are in the dark together, – near,
Yet far, – and fear
Drums on my ear
In that sage company drear.

How weak and little is the light,
All the universe of sight,
Love and delight,
Before the might,
If you love it not, of night.

Edward Thomas

The Warm and the Cold

Freezing dusk is closing
  Like a slow trap of steel
On trees and roads and hills and all
  That can no longer feel.
    But the carp is in its depth
      Like a planet in its heaven.
    And the badger in its bedding
      Like a loaf in the oven.
    And the butterfly in its mummy
      Like a viol in its case.
    And the owl in its feathers
      Like a doll in its lace.

Freezing dusk has tightened
  Like a nut screwed tight
On the starry aeroplane
  Of the soaring night.
    But the trout is in its hole
      Like a chuckle in a sleeper.
    The hare strays down the highway
      Like a root going deeper.
    The snail is dry in the outhouse
      Like a seed in a sunflower.
    The owl is pale on the gatepost
      Like a clock on its tower.

Moonlight freezes the shaggy world
  Like a mammoth of ice –
The past and the future
  Are the jaws of a steel vice.
    But the cod is in the tide-rip
      Like a key in a purse.
    The deer are on the bare-blown hill
      Like smiles on a nurse.
    The flies are behind the plaster
      Like the lost score of a jig.
    Sparrows are in the ivy-clump
      Like money in a pig.

Such a frost
  The flimsy moon
    Hast lost her wits.

    A star falls.

The sweating farmers
  Turn in their sleep
    Like oxen on spits.

Ted Hughes

Farewell to the Farm

The coach is at the door at last;
The eager children, mounting fast
And kissing hands, in chorus sing:
Good-bye, good-bye, to everything!

To house and garden, field and lawn,
The meadow-gates we swang upon,
To pump and stable, tree and swing,
Good-bye, good-bye, to everything!

And fare you well for evermore,
O ladder at the hayloft door,
O hayloft where the cobwebs cling,
Good-bye, good-bye, to everything!

Crack goes the whip, and off we go;
The trees and houses smaller grow;
Last, round the woody turn we swing:
Good-bye, good-bye, to everything!

Robert Louis Stevenson

Acknowledgements

James Campbell 'I will go with my father a-ploughing' from *The Field Day Anthology of Irish Writing* by permission of Field Day Publications; **Charles Causley** 'Riley' from *Collected Poems for Children* (Macmillan), by permission of David Higham Associates; **Gillian Clarke** 'Haymaking' from *Collected Poems*, by permission of Carcanet Press Limited; **Elizabeth Coatsworth** 'What Could Be Lovelier Than To Hear' by permission of the Estate of Elizabeth Coatsworth and Paterson Marsh Ltd; **Maura Dooley** 'Up on the Moors with Keeper' from *Sound Barrier: Poems 1982 – 2002* (2002), by permission of Bloodaxe Books, 'Net and River' by permission of the poet; **Carol Ann Duffy** 'A Crow and a Scarecrow' by permission of Faber & Faber; **Eleanor Farjeon** 'For a Dewdrop' from *Joan's Door* (Collins), by permission of David Higham Associates; **Seamus Heaney** 'Follower', 'Every Night I Glean and Raid', by permission of Faber & Faber; **Molly Holden** 'Hare' © Alan Holden 2004, by permission of Alan Holden; **Ted Hughes** 'A Lamb in the Storm', 'Weasels at Work', 'A March Calf', 'New Foal', 'The Warm and the Cold', by permission of Faber & Faber; **Jackie Kay** 'Sheep Shearing, Skye' from *Two's Company* (Blackie, 1992), by permission of Penguin Books Ltd; **Norman MacCaig** 'Fetching Cows', 'Summer Farm', from *Collected Poems*, published by Chatto & Windus, used by permission of the Random House Group Limited; **Hugh MacDiarmid** 'Perfect' from *Collected Poems*, by permission of Carcanet Press Limited; **George Mackay Brown** 'The Hawk' from *Selected Poems*, by permission of John Murray (Publishers) Ltd; **Walter de la Mare** 'The Huntsmen'

Glossary

bunnet: *cap*
cadows: *jackdaws*
corbie: *crow*
gean: *wild cherry*
lew: *shade*
machair: *beach*
minjies: *small minnows*
whipper-in: *the huntsman
 who looked after the hounds*